This book was made especially
for Nana's little guy!

My Nana loves me,
I know that!

More than a kitty
with a big, red hat.

More than an elephant standing on a ball...

or a happy, purple crab
that is oh, so small!

My Nana loves me,
that you'll see..

more than a little calf
looking at a bee!

More than an alligator
playing his trombone,

or a silly looking cow
singing with a microphone!

or a bunny that is skiing.
That would really be a hoot!

My Nana loves me,
that's no lie...

more than a lizard
with a suit and tie!

More than some horses
running in a race...

or a bunny with a snorkle
and a mask on his face!

More than a hippo,
standing on a scale...

or a doggy that is hiking
on a long, long trail!

More than a penguin
surfing on the sea,

When the stars shine bright...

or the sky is blue...

my Nana loves me,

that is TRUE! TRUE! TRUE!

My Nana Loves Me! by Sally Helmick North

Sally was born in Jackson, Michigan. She has lived all over the country with her husband, Fred. They have 3 grown children. She has written over 30 children's books and had her first book published in 2000. Sneaky Snail Stories are all sweet and simple rhyming books with really cute illustrations. You can see all the Sneaky Snail Stories at: www.sneakysnailstories.com

Other books by Sally:
Grandma and Grandpa Love You! (Many versions)
Mimi Loves You! (Many versions)
I Love Noah! (Many names available)
I Love Emma! (Many names available)
Noah Loves Animals (Many names available)
Emma Loves Animals (Many names available)

Search Amazon for "Personalized book for (child's name) by Sally Helmick North"
Or visit my website: www.kidsbookwithname.com

Made in the USA
Las Vegas, NV
28 November 2021

35505744R00017